PUFFIN BOOKS *Editor: Kaye Webb*

PONDER AND WILLIAM ON HOLIDAY

Ponder the pyjama-case was sitting on the spare-room bed looking fat and firm and pleased with himself. Ponder looked firm because he was stuffed with a pair of William's pyjamas, and he looked pleased because he had something very special to tell William.

'Do you know, William,' he began, 'I've got a secret.'

'Ssh –' said William. 'You mustn't say it out loud. Secrets are always whispered.'

Ponder crept across the eiderdown. He took a deep breath, his eyes grew as round as saucers, his whiskers began to twitch, his nose touched William's ear – 'We – are – going – to – the seaside,' he said slowly. 'Cousin Winifred is taking us to the seaside for seven whole days!'

Many readers will already know the sort of things that are likely to happen to Ponder and William at the seaside because of Barbara Softly's first book, but those who don't are in for a lot of fun with this gay and happy sequel.

Ponder and William On Holiday

Barbara Softly

With drawings by Diana John

Penguin Books

Penguin Books Ltd, Harmondsworth, Middlesex, England
Penguin Books Inc., 7110 Ambassador Road, Baltimore, Maryland 21207,
U.S.A.
Penguin Books Australia Ltd, Ringwood, Victoria, Australia

First published 1968
Reprinted 1971, 1973
Copyright © Barbara Softly, 1968

Made and printed in Great Britain by
Hazell Watson & Viney Ltd
Aylesbury, Bucks
Set in Monotype Bembo

For Gareth Reed,
Christopher and Martin Lambert,
Simon Beck and Karen Rogers

Contents

Ponder Does Some Packing

It was summer time and William had come to stay with Cousin Winifred, not for a weekend holiday as usual, but for a holiday of a whole week – seven whole days with Cousin Winifred, her three cats, Tigger, Ginnie and Marmalade, and of course Ponder.

Ponder was the pyjama-case, the panda pyjama-case who sat on the spare-room bed where William slept, looking fat and firm and pleased with himself. Ponder looked fat and firm because he was always stuffed with one pair of William's pyjamas – William brought another pair for himself whenever he came to stay – and Ponder looked pleased because this time he had something special to tell William.

He started telling him while William was unpacking his suitcase. There were socks and shoes, shirts and pants all over the floor, and his toothbrush was already in its mug on the window-sill.

Ponder's black eyes were shiny bright.

'Do you know, William,' he began. 'I've got a secret.'

'A secret?' asked William.

Ponder nodded. 'And it's – it's –'

'Ssh –' said William. 'You mustn't say it out loud. Secrets are always whispered.'

'Whispered? How do you do that?' asked Ponder.

William climbed on to the bed and sat very close to Ponder.

'Like this,' he said, and he took a deep breath, put his mouth against Ponder's ear and hissed, 'I've got a secret.'

'Have you?' Ponder shouted, and jumped away to the other side of the bed rubbing his ear with his paw.

'Sssh –' William said again. 'Now you try.'

Ponder crept across the eiderdown. He took a deep breath, his eyes grew as round as saucers, his whiskers began to twitch, his nose touched William's ear –

'It's – it's – phew – oo –' he snorted, and all the breath came out in one big rush.

'You're tickling,' William laughed. 'Start again.'

Ponder took another deep breath, but the breath kept wobbling up and down inside him making his whiskers twitch more than ever.

'Wig— wig— wig— wig – wig—' he squeaked.

'Go on,' William chuckled. 'Wig – what?'

'Wig-wig-wig-wigone –' Ponder exploded like a burst balloon, and he and William collapsed on the bed in a gurgling heap.

When they were able to sit up again, William made his face very straight and said, 'Don't whisper any more, Ponder, just tell me the secret.'

Ponder made his face straight too. He clasped his paws on his chest and stared at William's tooth mug on the window-sill, so that even his whiskers would not twitch.

'We – are – going – to – the – seaside,' he said slowly.

'The seaside!' William exclaimed, and he could not keep his face straight any longer. 'For a whole day, like we did before?'

Ponder shook his head and beamed at William, for this was the most important part of the secret.

'For seven whole days – Cousin Winifred is taking us to the seaside for a holiday for seven whole days!'

'Ponder!' William seized Ponder by the paws and whirled him round and round.

'Sing a song of summer time,
    A pocket full of apples,' he chanted.

'Sing a song of summer time,
    A bucket full of sand,' puffed Ponder, when

William had put him down again. 'That was a good secret, wasn't it?'

William did not answer. He was looking at his suitcase on the floor.

'I ought to start packing again,' he said. 'And you'll need a suitcase too, Ponder, if we stay for a whole week.'

Ponder shook his head. 'I don't want a suitcase.'

'Why not?' asked William.

'I've nothing to put in a suitcase. Suits go in suit-cases and packing goes in packing-cases. I want a packing-case.'

William wasn't sure what a packing-case was like.

'We had better go and ask Cousin Winifred,' he said.

So Ponder and William slid off the bed and ran downstairs to find Cousin Winifred – and Cousin Winifred knew exactly what a packing-case was like. She told them to go down the garden, open the garden shed, and there, behind the door, they would find a packing-case.

Ponder and William rushed out of the house, down the path between the lawn and the flower-beds, up the steps into the vegetable patch, past the seat under the apple tree where the three cats were sitting in the sun, and they lifted the latch on the door of the shed.

Creak – creak – went the door, and bump – as it hit something hard.

'Packing-case!' cried Ponder.

He scrambled in front of William and dragged out

a large square cardboard box with four flaps for a lid.

'It hasn't got a handle. It's not like a suitcase at all,' said William.

'Packing-cases don't have handles,' said Ponder, and he marched up the path to the house pulling his packing-case after him.

'There,' he said, when they were in the kitchen, 'now I can do my packing.'

William sat on the kitchen stool while Ponder trotted backwards and forwards filling his packing-case.

First he put in a box of fat, juicy currants – Ponder was very fond of currants – next a large red apple, then two slices of currant bread, one slice of brown bread, one thick slice of currant cake and, last of all, a packet of rice. Ponder did not really want the rice, but it filled up the corner by the apple. Then he looked round the kitchen to see if there was anything else he might need on his week's holiday by the sea.

Up on a hook by the sink hung Cousin Winifred's kitchen towel. It was a very old kitchen towel, grey and ragged at the edges, because Cousin Winifred was going to put out a bright clean new one when they went away in the morning.

Ponder took down the towel and stuffed it in the top of his packing-case.

'I might paddle and get my feet wet,' he said.

He and William tucked in the four flaps which made the lid, and together they carried the packing-

case out into the hall where it would be ready to go
to the seaside with them next day.

'I like packing,' said Ponder happily. 'We had
better go and do yours now.'

Ponder's Song of Summer Time

Sing a song of summer time,
A bucket in my hand,
A wooden spade for digging,
A smooth stretch of sand.
Here I plan my castle
To look across the sea,
To watch the shore for ships that sail
From other lands to me.

Sing a song of summer time,
A castle built of sand;
Four walls with four towers
Upon the seashore stand.
With pearly shells for windows,
A gateway made of stone,
My castle looks across the sea
And guards the shore alone.

Cousin Winifred's Kitchen Towel

The next morning the three cats, Tigger, Ginnie and Marmalade were sitting on the garden wall washing their paws. They were very glad that they were not going away with Ponder and William on holiday. Cousin Winifred's friend was coming to look after them and, as long as they had plenty to eat, plenty to drink, their baskets to sleep in, the garden to play in and the apple tree to climb, they were much happier at home.

'Good-bye house, good-bye garden, good-bye cats,' called Ponder, as he and William ran down the path and climbed into the taxi that was waiting to take them to the station.

Cousin Winifred's large suitcase, William's small suitcase and Ponder's packing-case were all stacked in front by the driver. Cousin Winifred, Ponder and William sat in a row on the back seat.

Ponder watched his packing-case carefully to see that it did not fall out of the taxi as they swung down the lane, on to the main road and into the village. He watched it when the porter carried it from the taxi to the platform on the station, and he watched it when the train came in and Cousin Winifred put it up on the rack with the other two suitcases. After that, Ponder forgot all about it, he was so busy watching

everything else out of the carriage window and listening to the song of the train.

'*Diddly – der, diddly – der, diddly – diddly – diddly – der,*' it sang faster and faster as it raced along its silver tracks on the way to the sea.

William liked the song of the train too, and so he and Ponder sang it together – '*diddly – der, diddly – der, diddly – diddly – diddly – der –*' until Cousin Winifred said that their throats must be dry with all that singing and gave them orange juice to drink with straws out of cardboard cartons.

Ponder particularly liked the bubbly noise made by the straw at the bottom of the carton when there wasn't any more orange juice left to drink.

At last, when the train stopped at a station it seemed that everybody was getting out. The doors of all the carriages went bang-bang-bang-bang.

Cousin Winifred carried the two suitcases, and Ponder and William, carrying the packing-case, followed her down the platform, down a long slope, round a corner – and then –

Ponder and William stood quite still in surprise. They had expected to see the sand and blue sea stretching away until it touched the sky. But there wasn't any sand and they could hardly see any sea for, right in front of them, was the largest boat they had ever seen. It was larger than a rowing boat, or a motor boat, or a sailing boat. It gleamed from end to end with green and white paint; there were white railings all round its sides, long brown seats on the decks, a red funnel and two thin shining masts on which the seagulls were perched in the sun.

Ponder and William suddenly felt very quiet and very good for they knew they were going on that boat, and that nothing quite so exciting had ever happened to them before. They tiptoed behind Cousin Winifred up the gangway on to the deck and they sat side by side on one of the brown seats by the white railings.

William squeezed Ponder's paw.

'It's a steamer,' he whispered.

'Yes,' said Ponder, and he tried to look as though he went on a steamer every day of his life.

When all the people had come on board and all the luggage had been put on deck, 'tu-whup, tu-whup,' went the steamer out of its red funnel, and 'ting-ting,

ting-ting,' went a little bell, and there came a strange
whirring noise from underneath their feet.

'Why – it's purring!' William exclaimed.

'Steamers always purr, like the cats,' said Ponder.

Louder and louder the steamer purred and headed
away for the sparkling open sea.

The wind ruffled Ponder's fur. It ruffled William's
hair until he put up the hood of his jacket to stop it
blowing down his neck, and the farther they went the
harder it blew.

'Ke-ow – ke-ow –' cried the seagulls, flying from
the masts and gliding round the steamer, 'ke-ow.'

However fast the boat sailed the seagulls were able to keep up with it. They hovered over the deck, their great wings flapping slowly, their bright eyes watching and their pale pink feet dangling from under their feathers.

'Ke – ow – we're – hun-gry –' they cried.

Ponder seized his packing-case and began unfastening the four cardboard flaps of the lid. He tugged at Cousin Winifred's kitchen towel and pulled out a piece of currant bread.

'Do you – think – seagulls will like – currants?' he puffed through the gusts of wind.

William nodded.

'Ke-ow –' cried a seagull, diving for Ponder's paw.

Before Ponder could stop him he had snatched the bread and gobbled it up while the other seagulls swooped eagerly round him.

William bounced up and down with excitement.

'Give me a piece – give me a piece. I want to see if they'll take it from me too. Hurry, Ponder, hurry.'

Ponder hurried, and he hurried so much that the kitchen towel flew out of the packing-case.

'Ke-ow!' cried the seagulls.

'Phew – oo!' cried the wind.

'My t – o – w – el!' cried Ponder, and Cousin Winifred's kitchen towel went soaring up in the air.

It hovered over the deck like a giant seagull. A nasty brown patch where William had wiped his muddy hands showed up against the blue of the sky,

'Keow!' shrieked the seagulls, as it flapped towards them.

It wriggled over the funnel, swooped over the railings, and then with a little twist went floating up – up – up.

'It's got a hole in it,' said Ponder.

And it had, and the hole caught on the mast at the other end of the steamer – and the towel streamed out behind the boat like a ragged grey flag.

William went very red.

'It's not our towel,' he said, and he turned his back on it.

'Not ours at all,' said Ponder.

And they both bent over the packing-case and tried to pretend that they did not know anything about the dirty kitchen towel that was flying from the mast of the shining green and white steamer.

They gave the rest of the bread and the currant cake to the seagulls and sat down quietly on the long brown seat with Cousin Winifred.

Cousin Winifred began to tell them about the place where they were going for their holiday. It was an island, and it had the sea all round it. There were hills, trees and farms, white cliffs and sandy beaches. They were staying all by themselves with her in a little stone cottage in a lane that went down to the shore where there were rocks and paddling pools full of seaweed, shrimps and crabs.

Ponder thought he liked the sound of the Island very much indeed. He clasped his paws on his chest and smiled.

'Will there be any shops?' he asked William.

'Why?' said William.

Ponder's dark eyes twinkled.

'I might want to buy a towel, in case I paddle and get my feet wet,' he said.

Ponder's Song of the Steamers

Some steamers carry oranges,
Peaches, lemons, dates,
Nectarines,
Tangerines,
Bananas packed in crates.

Some steamers carry chocolate,
Coffee, sugar, spice,
Monkey-nuts,
Coco-nuts,
Semolina, rice.

Our steamer carries passengers,
Cases in their hands;
Holidays,
Happy days
Across in other lands.

The Tree That Talked

When Ponder woke up in the morning he remembered where he was. He was on holiday with William and Cousin Winifred. On holiday on the Island, staying in a little stone cottage with grass all round it, a stone wall round the grass, and a big chestnut tree growing in the middle of the grass.

'Holiday,' said Ponder.

He scrambled off the bed and looked out of the window. There was the chestnut tree with the sun shining through its leaves making patterns like little umbrellas all over the bedroom floor.

'I'm going to explore,' said Ponder to himself, and he went out into the passage.

At one end of the passage he could hear Cousin Winifred humming in the kitchen. At the other end of the passage the front door stood wide open showing the grass, the trees and the blue sky beyond.

Ponder tiptoed through the front door and down the steps on to the lawn. Everything was very quiet, not a sound except the faint wash-wash of the sea at the end of the lane, and a seagull calling 'ke-ow, ke-ow,' as it swooped over the water.

Ponder ran across the grass to the wall. He dug his toes into the rough stones and climbed up – up until

he could see over the top into the dusty lane below.
There wasn't a sound. All the other little stone
cottages were silent, their doors were shut, but the
wind was blowing their bright cotton curtains
through their open windows into the sunshine.

'Good morning,' said a voice behind Ponder.

Ponder turned round.

'Good morning,' he said politely, although he
couldn't see anyone who might have spoken to
him.

'Good morning,' said the voice again.

Ponder peered over into the lane, he looked up and

down the lane, and he looked at the row of little stone cottages.

'Good morning,' he said very firmly.

'Two pints of milk today, please,' said the voice.

Ponder slid off the wall.

'It must be someone talking to the milkman,' he said, and he walked to the front gate.

There was no sign of the milkman anywhere, and there were no signs of empty milk bottles standing outside any of the doors in the lane. In fact, one or two doors had full milk bottles standing on their steps, which made it seem to Ponder that the milkman had called already.

'I can see you – I can see you – I can see you,' chuckled the voice merrily.

'I can't see you,' Ponder shouted, and he ran up the path to the house to see what William was doing, because he felt sure that it must be William who was talking to him.

But when he reached the steps he could hear William in the kitchen with Cousin Winifred.

Ponder looked thoughtful and puzzled.

'It's not William,' he said. 'It's not Cousin Winifred, it's not the milkman, it's not the postman or anyone in the lane at all – so – who can it be?'

Very slowly he went down the steps again and stared round the garden, at the grass, the wall and the big chestnut tree.

Suddenly the chestnut tree gave a little shake as if it was beginning to dance.

'Cock-a-doodle-do,
My dame has lost her shoe,
My master's lost his fiddling stick
And I don't know what to do,'

it sang. 'Ha-ha-ha-ha-ha!' and there was a great gale of laughter which shook the branches so much that little twigs and baby chestnuts came tumbling through the leaves to the ground.

Ponder turned and raced indoors.

'William, William,' he cried excitedly. 'Come out at once. There's a tree in the garden that talks.'

William came running from the kitchen.

'Where, Ponder, where?' he asked.

'There,' said Ponder proudly, and he pointed with his paw at the chestnut tree. 'It said "Good morning" to me and lots of other things as well.'

William stared at the chestnut tree and then he walked all round it. The chestnut tree stood quite still, not a leaf quivered, not a branch shook and not a word did it say.

Ponder put out a paw and patted the trunk of the tree.

'How do you do, tree?' he said. 'Good morning.'

'Good morning, tree,' said William.

'He – ll – o,' said the tree very quietly.

'There,' whispered Ponder. 'It does talk.'

William nodded and his eyes were as bright as Ponder's as they both crept closer and peered up into the green branches.

Then William stretched out his foot and started to climb on to the lowest green branch. Ponder followed him.

> 'Cock-a-doodle-do,
>   My dame has lost her shoe,
>   My master's lost his fiddling stick
>   And I don't know what to do,'

sang the voice above their heads.

All the leaves began to dance up and down and showers of baby chestnuts fell past Ponder and William to the grass.

Suddenly the tree rustled.

'Good morning,' it said, and this time the voice was right behind William's ear.

'Hello,' and the voice was down at William's feet. 'Two pints of milk today, please.'

William leaned over the branch and then, nearly touching his nose, what do you think he saw? A large bird with a curved beak, shining eyes and a plume of feathers on its head.

'Ponder!' William squealed. 'It's a parrot – I know it's a parrot because I've seen them at the zoo. It's not the tree talking, it's a real live parrot.'

Ponder stared and stared, and the parrot put its head on one side, scuttled along to the end of the branch and said – 'Hello.'

Then it scuttled back again, and fixed Ponder with its beady eyes.

'Two pints of milk today, please, ha-ha-ha-ha-ha!'

'Ha-ha-ha-ha-ha!' Ponder laughed too, which so surprised the parrot that it stood on its toes, flapped its wings and shrieked 'Caw!'

'Let's go and tell Cousin Winifred,' said William.

So he and Ponder slid down the branch and hurried indoors to tell Cousin Winifred about the talking chestnut tree, which wasn't a talking chestnut tree after all, but a real live parrot.

And Cousin Winifred knew more about the parrot than they did. She said he had lived there for years and years, far longer than she could remember, that he belonged to the lady in the next stone cottage, and that his name was Hector.

'I think we might see Hector again if he lives in that chestnut tree,' said Ponder, as they sat down to breakfast.

And William thought so, too.

Ponder's Song of the Parrot

Polly put the kettle on,
Polly put the kettle on,
Polly put the kettle on,
We'll all have tea.
But Polly was a parrot
And she couldn't put the kettle on;
Polly was a parrot
And Polly said to me –
You must put the kettle on,
You must put the kettle on,
Fill it up with water
And boil it for our tea –
I did as Polly told me,
I did as Polly told me,
I heated up the teapot
And put in spoons for three.
I put in one for Polly,
I put in one for Polly,
Put in one to please the pot
And put in one for me.
I had the water boiling,
I had the water boiling,

Tipped it in the teapot
And left for minutes three.
Polly put the kettle on,
Polly put the kettle on,
Polly put the kettle on,
We've all had tea.
Though Polly was a parrot
And she couldn't put the kettle on,
Polly taught me how to make
A real cup of tea!

Going Shopping

The sea was just at the bottom of the lane below the little stone cottage, and Cousin Winifred said that before they all went shopping, they would go down to the shore to see what the sea was doing.

'If it's in,' William said, 'we shan't be able to go on the beach yet because there won't be any beach to go on.'

Paw-in-hand Ponder and William raced ahead down the lane so that they would be the first to see the sea.

'In – it's in!' William cried, as they turned the corner and there was the sea, smooth and blue, sending wavelets lapping against the wall which stopped it from splashing over on to their feet.

'There's sand when it's out,' said William. 'Sand and rocks and pools with shrimps in them. Cousin Winifred said that when she was a little girl she used to catch shrimps in shrimping-nets and put them in her bucket full of sea water.'

'What did she do with the shrimps when they were in her bucket?' asked Ponder.

'Counted them and put them back in the sea,' said William.

'O-oh.' Ponder looked thoughtful. 'If we had shrimping-nets we could go shrimping too.'

'Yes,' said William, 'and if we had buckets we could put our shrimps in the buckets and count them.'

'Yes,' said Ponder, 'and if we went shrimping with shrimping-nets and put our shrimps in buckets and counted them, we should have to paddle in the rock-pools and we'd get our feet wet and – I haven't got a towel. We lost mine on the steamer.'

'But –' went on William, 'we could ask Cousin Winifred to buy you one, and shrimping-nets for us and buckets.'

'And spades,' said Ponder. 'We might want to build castles and boats like we did last time.'

Ponder and William ran back up the lane to Cousin

Winifred, and Cousin Winifred wrote at the end of her shopping list, after the apples and carrots and lettuce – two buckets, two shrimping-nets, one towel.

'Red, please,' Ponder whispered in William's ear.

The shop at the top of the lane was very small, but it seemed to sell everything there was to sell. It had two windows and two doors. In the first window there were packets of tea and sugar, tins of fruit and meat, and boxes of biscuits; outside the first door there were sacks of potatoes, boxes of apples, lettuces and tomatoes. In the second window there were bathing costumes and caps, tea-cloths and scarves; outside the second door there were buckets and spades, rubber rings, toy boats and picture postcards, and shrimping-nets.

Cousin Winifred went in that door first, and she bought two buckets, two spades, two shrimping-

nets, and then she asked for a towel. Ponder held his breath while the shop-lady pulled out a drawer full of towels, for he could not see a red one anywhere. But down at the bottom of the drawer William caught sight of a striped one. It was green, yellow, red and blue.

'It's like the deck-chairs on the beach,' he whispered to Ponder.

Ponder was so pleased that he chose that one and hung it round his neck like a scarf.

While Cousin Winifred went on talking to the shop-lady, Ponder and William, clutching their buckets, spades and shrimping-nets, wandered out

into the sun to look at the boats and picture postcards. Suddenly Ponder tugged at William's arm.

'There's a butterfly in that window with all the
biscuits and tea and things,' he said.

William stopped looking at the boats and picture
postcards and stared at the shop window. Ponder was
right. Fluttering against the glass was a pale yellow
butterfly.

'It flew in there and now it can't get out,' said
William. 'It thinks the glass is the open door. It won't
find anything to eat in there. Butterflies don't eat
biscuits and tea and sugar.'

'We could catch it and put it out in the sun again,'
said Ponder.

Ponder and William peered through the doorway.
The shop was empty. It was dark after the brightness
of the lane and smelt of cheese, ham and dog biscuits.
The counter was clean and white with glass covers
over the slices of meat and bacon. At each end of the
counter starting from the floor, were two huge piles
of tins. They were the tallest piles of tins that Ponder
and William had ever seen, all the tins balanced
carefully going up almost to the ceiling, thinner and
thinner until there was only one tin alone at the top.
For a moment Ponder and William almost forgot the
butterfly while they gazed at the beautiful piles, one
of soup, the other of baked bean tins.

'There it is!' Ponder shouted, for the butterfly
had flown from the window to flutter over the
counter.

'Catch it in our shrimping-nets!' cried William.

He and Ponder dropped their buckets and spades on the floor and darted after the butterfly with shrimping-nets raised. Round the counter, round the shop, over the tops of the piles of tins, back to the window fluttered the butterfly with Ponder and William close behind. Round the counter, round the shop, over the tops of the tins, back to the window – round the counter – round the –

'It's all right, Ponder,' William panted. 'It's going out of the door –' and they raced after it.

But Ponder and William did not go out of the door with the yellow butterfly – they tripped over their buckets and spades, and the shrimping-nets went – smack – into the beautiful pile of soup tins.

'Ponder – oh!'

'Oh – William!'

Bump-bump-bumpety-bump-bumpety-bumpety-bump-bump!

Ponder and William sat rubbing their bruised fingers and knees while more tins clattered and tumbled past them – bump-bumpety-bump.

Then they heard voices. William seized his shrimping-net, bucket and spade; Ponder seized his shrimping-net, bucket and spade, and wound his towel tightly round his neck. They fled and hid behind the baked beans at the other end of the counter.

Ponder stood on tiptoe and peered through a gap in the baked beans. Cousin Winifred and the shop-lady were hurrying through the door. Cousin

Winifred looked at the soup tins all over the floor, she looked round the shop and she looked very hard at the pile of baked bean tins. Ponder shut his eyes.

'If I can't see her, she can't see me,' he thought.

When Ponder opened his eyes Cousin Winifred was pushing the tins nearer the wall, and the shop-lady was saying that she would not put them up in a pile in case they fell down again, but she would arrange them on a shelf later.

Cousin Winifred bought two of the tins of soup. Then she went outside with the shop-lady and bought apples, oranges, carrots and a lettuce, and then they both went back into the other part of the shop.

Ponder and William crept from behind the baked beans and, with their shrimping-nets over their shoulders, they tiptoed into the sunshine.

There was no sign of the yellow butterfly any-where, so Ponder and William stood side by side choosing a picture postcard for William to send home to his mother and father and waiting very quietly for Cousin Winifred to finish her shopping.

When she came out of the shop, Cousin Winifred didn't say anything at all – but she didn't let them go shrimping that day.

Ponder's Song of the Lane

Under the trees
In the lane in the shade,
The light is dappled
Like an apple glade.
Thick grow the ferns
In the lane-side ditches,
Tall grow the foxgloves,
Thimbles for witches;
High climb the woodbine
And traveller's joy,
Creeps on the sea wall
Roving sailor-boy.
Who lives in the lane
By the lapping sea?
Dragonfly, butterfly,
And bumble-bee.

William and the Ponder-Paddle

Ponder and William were sitting on the seashore. It was hot, so hot that the sea seemed too lazy to take itself away from the beach, and the little waves were plopping softly one by one on to the warm sand.

It was so hot that Cousin Winifred had made them both sun hats out of sheets of her newspaper. The hats looked like paper boats. William wore his with the points over his nose and neck; Ponder wore his with the points over his ears because it sat more firmly on his head that way.

Ponder ran his paws into the warm sand. His bucket and spade were by his side, his striped towel and shrimping-net behind him. It was too hot to build castles, too hot to catch shrimps if there had been any shrimps to catch, but there weren't, because the sea was still lapping over the rocks where the shrimp pools lay.

'But it's not too hot for swimming,' said William. 'I'm going swimming.'

He put his hat under a stone, jumped up and ran down to the edge of the water. One little wave flopped over on to his toes.

'It's warm,' he called to Ponder. 'Come and watch me swim.'

Ponder got up slowly. He walked down the beach with his paws behind his back trailing his striped towel after him, and he stood just out of reach of the little waves watching William.

William waded in until the sea was up to his knees. Then he put his hands on the sand and splashed his legs about.

'Is that swimming?' asked Ponder.

'Nearly,' said William. 'Now watch. This is swimming.'

William took his hands off the sand, splashed wildly with his legs and arms, and nearly disappeared under a wave.

'That was swimming,' he said.

'Looked like sinking to me,' said Ponder. 'You didn't swim very far.'

He dropped his hat and towel and padded forward until the sea was washing over his feet. He raised one foot and shook it, raised the other foot and shook it.

'Wet,' he said, and wriggled his toes in the squelching sand.

'Are you coming in?' asked William.

'Yes,' said Ponder, and he walked straight into the water.

The water splashed up his black legs, up – up – and touched the black band on his chest. Ponder took a deep breath, he pushed out his paws and he glided into the water.

Paddle – paddle – splash – phew! Paddle – paddle – splash – phew!

William stared and then he started to laugh. He sat down in the water and he laughed and laughed.

'You look like an elephant, Ponder,' he chuckled.

'This is how elephants swim,' Ponder spluttered, and he went on.

Paddle – paddle – splash – phew! Paddle – paddle – splash – phew! And he was moving, actually moving!

'Ponder!' William cried. 'Are you swimming? Really swimming?'

'Of course I am.' Paddle – paddle – splash – phew!

William scrambled to his feet and he splashed through the water until it was nearly up to his chest too.

'You haven't got your feet on the bottom?'

'No,' said Ponder, and there were his back feet going up and down, up and down.

'You haven't got your paws on the bottom?'

'No,' said Ponder, and there were his paws going paddle, paddle, paddle, paddle.

'Why have you got your mouth open?'

'Because I don't want to snort water up my nose, of course.'

And there was Ponder's head just above the water with his mouth going phew! every time he puffed the air in and out.

'Ponder!' William cried. 'Show me – show me how to swim. What sort of a swim is it?'

'My own swim,' said Ponder. He stopped swimming and stood up; the water streamed from his fur and the end of his nose. His eyes were shiny bright. 'It's a Ponder-paddle.'

William jumped up and down with excitement.

'What do I do, Ponder? What do I do? Teach me the Ponder-paddle.'

Ponder suddenly looked very important and pleased with himself.

'Keep your fingers together, like paws,' he said.

'Yes,' said William.

'Paddle your arms up and down – slowly – and paddle your legs up and down – slowly.'

'Yes.'

'And breathe through your mouth. Puff all the air and water out – phew!'

'Yes,' said William, but he knew that was going to be very difficult indeed because no one had ever let him breathe through his mouth before. He was always being told to keep his mouth shut and breathe through his nose.

'Are you sure that's right?' he asked, for he wondered what Cousin Winifred would say.

'Yes,' said Ponder. 'Go on, do the Ponder-paddle.'

William pushed his hands forward and slid into the water. He was so busy trying to keep his mouth open and paddle his hands like paws that he forgot all about his legs and suddenly found that they were paddling themselves.

'I'm swim– –' he began, swallowed a mouthful of water and came up coughing.

'Go on,' said Ponder. 'Try it again.'

William stopped spluttering and tried it again, and he swam the Ponder-paddle, not very far, but he kept his feet and hands off the bottom and puffed hard

with his mouth. He and Ponder swam side by side –
paddle – paddle – splash – phew! Paddle – paddle –
splash – phew!

When Cousin Winifred called them up the beach
and they had both been rubbed warm with their
towels – and Ponder was sitting in the hot sun to
finish drying off his fur – William said,

'I like the Ponder-paddle, but it's the funniest kind
of swim I've ever seen.'

Ponder twitched his ears and settled his sun hat on
his head.

'But it's better to swim any sort of swim than not
be able to swim at all,' he said.

And Cousin Winifred agreed.

Ponder's Song of Swimming

Some do the breast-stroke,
Some do the crawl,
Some do the side-stroke,
Some do them all;
Some dive like swallows
To glide in waters dim,
Some do the back-stroke –
   I just swim –
For it's better to swim
Any sort of swim,
Than not to swim at all!

Some tread the water,
Some like to lie
On their backs a-floating
Others splashing by;
Some only sunbathe
To pickle every limb,
Some peel all over –
  I just swim –
For it's better to swim
Any sort of swim,
Than not to swim at all!

What Ponder Caught in his Shrimping-Net

The sea had gone out at last. It had gone so far that it looked as though there was only a narrow strip of blue water left for the ships to sail on between the sand and the sky. To Ponder it seemed that there were miles of sand between him and the strip of blue; miles of hard wet sand, ridged by the little waves that had flopped upon it, and scattered with shells and clusters of rocks where the shrimp pools lay.

'Let's go shrimping now,' he said to William.

Leaving their spades and towels with Cousin Winifred, Ponder and William took their buckets and shrimping-nets and set off for the rocks. Halfway across the sand William bent down and picked up a shell.

'Look at that, Ponder,' he said. 'It's just like a little boat. It's even got a seat in it.'

Heads together, they looked at the boatlike shell on William's hand.

'And look at this,' said Ponder, bending down and picking up a tiny yellow shell.

'And this!' William pounced on a large shell which curled to a point at one end. 'This is a listening shell.' He pressed the shell close to his ear. 'You can hear the sea in it.' And he gave it to Ponder to try.

As Ponder listened, his eyes grew round with

surprise, for he could hear a hissing, roaring sound like the sea washing on a far-away shore.

'Can we keep it?' he asked. 'Then I can listen to the sea whenever I like when we get back home.'

'We'll keep them all,' said William, and he dropped the shells into his bucket.

By the time they had reached the rock pools, William's pail was nearly full of shells.

'We'll use yours for the shrimps,' he said to Ponder.

Ponder leaned over a rock and dipped his pail into the water. The sun glistened on the sand at the bottom of the pool and Ponder was sure there would be shrimps in the cool, still shallows.

'I'm going to shrimp here,' he said.

William clambered carefully over the slippery

seaweed and dropped with a splash into another pool.

'I'm shrimping here,' he called.

He pushed his net through the water, paddling slowly after it.

Ponder stood on the rock by his pool and poked with his net among the trails of seaweed.

Push – push – scoop.

He drew up the glistening net with sand, seaweed and water trickling through its holes. He peered into it, but there were no shrimps, not even a crab. Ponder tried again.

Push – push – scoop.

Sand, water and seaweed glistened and trickled again. Ponder peered – and this time, this time, something shone in the corner of the net. It shone like gold.

'William – quick – quick – I've caught something!' Ponder cried. 'It's a goldfish.'

'A goldfish!' William gasped, as he splashed to Ponder's side. 'Where?'

'Look.' Ponder pointed with his paw at the gleam of gold.

William peered, and very carefully held the net in Ponder's pail of water – but the goldfish did not move.

'Tip it in the bucket,' he said.

Ponder turned the net upside-down, and the goldfish fell with a plop to the bottom of the pail. They both stared in surprise, first at the pail and then at each other, for the goldfish was a ring, a bright golden ring with a shining stone in the middle.

'We'd better show it to Cousin Winifred,' said William.

Hurriedly they picked up their pail of shells and, with their shrimping-nets under their arms, they raced back up the beach.

When Cousin Winifred saw the ring she said it might be valuable and that someone had probably lost it while bathing when the sea was in. She also said that they ought to take it to the police-station at once.

William combed his hair and put on his pullover and sandals. Ponder shook the sand out of his fur. Neither of them had ever been to a police-station before and they did not want to look untidy. Paw-in-hand, keeping close to Cousin Winifred, they set off up the lane to find the police-station.

The police-station was exactly like all the other

stone cottages in the lane, only it had a blue lamp outside and a notice-board with pictures on it. There were
more pictures on the walls inside. Under the window
there was a large desk and behind the desk there was

a policeman. Ponder suddenly became very shy and
tried to hide behind William's legs.

The policeman was very friendly. He looked at the
ring and he listened to Cousin Winifred, and then he
wrote down Cousin Winifred's name and address in
a book on the desk.

'But Ponder found it really,' William burst out,
standing on tiptoe and trying to see over the top of
the desk.

'Did he?' said the policeman. 'That was very clever of him. Where is he?'

Ponder hid his face and kept quite, quite still. But the policeman leaned right down and squeezed one of Ponder's paws.

'Well done, Ponder,' he smiled.

Ponder did not say a word all the way home, but when he and William had had their supper, cleaned their teeth, and were getting ready for bed, he said,

'That was a nice policeman.'

'Policemen are always nice,' said William.

'Do you think, do you think –' Ponder began, his eyes growing shiny bright with excitement. 'Do you think they have pandas in the police?'

William thought. 'They have dogs,' he said at last. 'Police dogs, and they might have pandas as well.'

'I should like to be a police panda,' said Ponder happily.

He curled up under the eiderdown and went to sleep, dreaming that he was a police panda with a dark blue helmet perched on the top of his head.

Ponder's Song of the Shell

I have a secret,
A secret to tell you,
A secret to whisper
Alone in your ear.
Only a whisper,
Listen, oh, listen,
Only a whisper
Which no one will hear.

The secret I tell you,
I heard from a seashell;
The sea tells its secrets
For seashells to hear.
Come, you shall listen,
Listen, oh, listen,
Pressing a seashell
Up close to your ear.

The House in the Garden

In the garden of the stone cottage there was a shed. It was something like the shed Cousin Winifred had under her apple tree only it looked even more like a little house.

Its back leaned against the rough garden wall. Its roof was covered with honeysuckle. In the front there were two windows, one each side of the door, and along under the door and windows there was a very wide step which had a low white railing round the edge broken by a tiny gate.

'It is a house,' said William, when he and Ponder were in the garden after breakfast. 'Cousin Winifred says it's a summer-house. You put chairs on the step part and sit in the sun.'

Ponder looked at the sun shining on the step part.

'There aren't any chairs there now,' he said.

'They're inside, I expect,' said William, and he stood on tiptoe and peered through the window.

Ponder tried to peer too, but he wasn't tall enough, and when he grew tired of tugging at William's pullover and watching him rub the dirty window with his handkerchief, he went up to the door of the summer-house and wriggled the handle. The handle moved and so did the door.

'William!' he cried. 'Come quickly. It's open!'

The door swung inwards and the sunlight streamed through. Ponder and William stood smiling at each other for the summer-house was full of chairs, little

green wooden chairs, striped deck-chairs, striped upright chairs, and it was full of other things as well – a round table, a lawn-mower, a wheel-barrow, a broom, garden forks, spades and hoes, lumpy sacks and a row of bottles and jars along a dusty shelf at the back.

'We could turn it into a real house,' said William. 'Take everything out and put the chairs on the step part –'

'And sweep the floor –' went on Ponder.

'And – polish the windows –'

'And put flowers on the table –'

'And dust the shelf and – and perhaps Cousin Winifred might let us have dinner out here and –'

'And tea?' Ponder raised a hopeful eyebrow.

William heaved a sigh of happiness.

'Let's start now,' he said.

Ponder and William started. They left the lawn-mower and the lumpy sacks in one corner because they were too heavy to move. They dragged the wheel-barrow on to the grass and filled it with the chairs they did not want. Three of the brightest chairs and the round table they set out on the step part in the sun, and one green wooden chair William kept to stand on to clean the windows.

Ponder took the broom and went inside the

summer-house to sweep the floor. He closed the door behind him.

'It's just like a real house, William,' he called. 'There's a bolt on the door and we can slide it along and shut ourselves in –'

'Don't slide the bolt, Ponder,' said William.

'Why not?' asked Ponder, and he did!

William rattled the door handle.

'Pull back the bolt, Ponder,' he said.

'Can't,' said Ponder. 'It's stuck.'

'Pull it back at once.'

Ponder looked at the bolt and he looked at the warm sun shining through the windows into the little house.

'I like it in here,' he said.

William climbed on to the green wooden chair and peered through the window with the sun.

'Pull the bolt back,' he called.

Ponder put his paws on the bolt. He pulled and wriggled and tugged, but the bolt would not move. It really had stuck after all.

'If you open the window I can come in and help,' William went on, tapping on the glass.

Ponder padded across the floor and stood on tiptoe. His eyes were shiny bright.

'Can't,' he said. 'Not tall enough.' And he sat on the lumpy sacks in the corner and closed his eyes.

'What are you doing?' William asked.

'Thinking,' said Ponder, 'and it's going to be a very long think.'

It was a very long think indeed and William grew tired of waiting.

'Well?' he asked, when Ponder jumped up and ran to the window.

'I've thought,' Ponder began slowly, 'that I'm not tall enough to open the window. If I had something to stand on then I'd be tall enough to open the window, but there's nothing in here to stand on, so – if you give me one of those green wooden chairs, then I can stand on it and open the window. That's what I've thought.'

William was silent for a little while. 'But I can't, Ponder,' he said. 'If you can't open the window or the door, how can I give you a chair?'

'Oh,' said Ponder, and he turned his back and stood looking at the row of bottles and jars on the shelf.

'Ponder!' said William suddenly. 'Is there an oil-can on the shelf? You could put some oil on the bolt and then I know it would slide back.'

Most of the bottles and jars had writing on them and Ponder couldn't read.

'How do you spell oil?' he asked.

It was William who had to think then. He knew how to spell William and Ponder and words like dog and cat, but those words seemed to have some sort of shape about them and oil had no shape at all. The more he said it out loud and the more Ponder called it back to him, the less it sounded like a word and became just a noise – oil – oil – oil.

'I could try a bit of everything,' said Ponder, beaming at the bottles and jars with their pictures of fat, red tomatoes, green cabbages and well-fed caterpillars, and he lifted down a large, black jar. He began singing to himself.

'If it's cabbages you're wanting,
    Or a carrot or a bean,
    Or a fat and juicy marrow
    Striped with yellow and with green;
    If it's turnip tops or parsley,
    Pods of peas and spinach too,
    I will dig them up or pick them
    Just as proper gardeners do.'

'There, Ponder, there!' William cried through the window. 'That's an oil-can, with the spout on it, behind the jar.'

Ponder put back the jar and picked up the oil-can.

It had a long, silvery spout and was something like a very thin coffee-pot.

'Tip it on the bolt,' William went on excitedly, and he jumped down from his chair.

Ponder tipped the oil-can and a thick stream of blue-green oil oozed all over the bolt. Ponder oozed oil on top of the bolt, underneath the bolt and each side of the bolt, and then he pulled at the bolt – and it came undone easily.

'There,' said William, as they stood face to face in the open door. 'But don't you ever shut yourself in anywhere again for there might not be an oil-can next time.'

And on the oil-can were the letters OIL – and William still did not think they made a word of much shape. Do you?

Ponder's Song of the Garden Shed

If it's bottles you are wanting,
Or an oil-can or a jar,
Or a mower or a barrow,
I can tell you where they are.
If it's forks and spades for digging,
Hoes for hoeing up the weeds,
Shears for trimming grassy edges,
Or a box to sow your seeds;
If it's just a pair of scissors
To snip flowers that are dead,
I can tell you where to find them —
They are in the garden shed.

The Punch and Judy Show

At the far end of the beach there was the pier where the shining green and white steamers tied up to land their passengers. The pier was long and narrow. It ran out into the sea until it reached water deep enough for the steamers to sail on. At high tide there was water underneath it all the way, green in the shadows and glistening with the sunlight that fell between the wooden planks; but at low tide, there was mostly sand, and it was some of the best sand on the whole of the beach.

Here there were deck-chairs for hire, white wooden rafts to paddle in the shallows, and a man who built castles, not the sort of castles that Ponder and William built out of upturned buckets, but models of real castles, models of animals and models of the green and white steamers all made out of the sand. He kept his cap by his side and people threw pennies into it from the seawall above. Right under the seawall, where they were sheltered from the wind, were the donkeys who gave the children rides along the beach for sixpence.

Early one afternoon, Ponder and William, having thrown pennies to the man who was now building a submarine, and patted the donkeys who were not yet

saddled up, suddenly saw something on the beach that they had never seen before.

'It's a little house,' said Ponder, and it looked like a little house only it was too tall and too thin for any-one to live in.

'I think it's a tent,' said William, and it really looked like a tent for it was striped red and white with a pointed roof like the row of bathing tents behind them.

'It's got a hole in the front,' said Ponder, as they went nearer.

'I know what it is!' William cried, jumping up and down. 'I know what it is! It's a Punch and Judy Show! I saw one at a party last Christmas.'

Ponder stared from the red and white tent to William's red, excited face.

'I don't know what a Punch and Judy Show is,' he said.

'It – it's a play – a story –' William went on breathlessly. 'There's a man in the tent and he makes up a play about Punch and Judy, and Punch and Judy come through the hole part and talk – and there's a dog and a baby and – and – a policeman.'

'A policeman?' asked Ponder, his black ears twitching. 'I should like to see the policeman. May we watch the Punch and Judy Show?'

William nodded, and as soon as they saw other children running along the beach to the red and white tent, they ran too, jumping over sandcastles and bathing costumes laid out to dry, in their hurry to find a good place to stand.

When all the children were crowded round, the tent shook and a head popped up through the opening and little hands pushed back the curtains.

'Hello, everybody,' said a funny cracked voice, and all the children laughed. 'Hello, everybody,' it said again. 'I'm Punch.'

Ponder's eyes grew as round as saucers.

'It sounds just like Hector the parrot,' he whispered to William.

'Ssh,' William said.

And Punch looked like Hector, too, in his bright striped clothes with his hooked nose, strutting up and down the platform of the red and white tent.

'Hello, everyone,' said another voice. 'I'm Punch's wife, Judy.' And up came a gaily dressed doll who strutted up and down with Punch.

'And this is our baby,' said Judy, and she showed all the children a tiny doll in her arms. 'And Punch is very unkind to our baby – he throws her out of the window.'

'No!' cried the watching children.

'Yes!' cried Judy. 'But Dog Toby brings her back

again. Toby – Toby –' she called. 'Dog Toby where are you?' And she peered over the edge of the platform down among the children.

Ponder and William and all the other children stood up on tiptoe, and there was Dog Toby sitting at the foot of the tent with a wide blue frill round his neck.

'Toby – Dog Toby –' Punch shouted as he looked over the platform as well.

'Woof – woof –' barked Dog Toby.

'He's real!' Ponder squeaked. 'He's a real dog!'

'Ssh!' said William.

'And when Dog Toby brings the baby back,' went on Judy, running along the platform, 'he fetches the policeman and the policeman whacks Punch on the head for being so unkind to the baby – and here is the policeman.'

'Ooh!' went up from the children, as a large blue policeman moved slowly on to the platform.

Ponder was so excited that he couldn't keep still at William's side and he began edging his way through the children until he was as close to the tent as he could get.

'And I whack Punch over the head. Like this!' said the policeman, and whack! went his stick on Punch's head.

'And I whack him back!' cried Punch. 'Whack! Whack!'

Everyone shrieked with laughter as Punch and the policeman whacked each other to and fro.

'And now –' said Punch, when he was nearly out of breath. 'We'll start the play.'

He leaned over the edge of the platform and saw Ponder staring at him.

'Hello,' he said. 'Hello – hello – hello. Who are you?'

And he sounded so much like Hector that Ponder could only stand and stare.

'Hello!' shouted Punch, and he brought his stick down whack! on Ponder's head.

Ponder sat down suddenly in the sand.

'Woof – woof –' barked Dog Toby – and he picked up Ponder in his mouth and scampered off behind the tent with him.

There was a great 'Oh' of delight from all the children – all except William. William forgot it was a play, he forgot there was a man in the tent pretending to be Punch, Judy and the policeman, he forgot everything except that Dog Toby had run away with Ponder.

'Ponder!' he cried.

He jumped over the laughing children. Pushing and wriggling past, he dashed up to the red and white tent and banged it with his fists.

'Where's Ponder?' he shouted. 'Dog Toby, what have you done with my panda? Give Ponder back at once, Dog Toby!'

The little tent rocked backwards and forwards.

Suddenly, the policeman came up on the platform.

'Oh dear, oh dear,' he boomed. 'What a dreadful thing to happen! Dog Toby is very sorry indeed. He really thought it was the baby Punch had whacked on the head and he brought your Ponder round by mistake. Here he is, safe and sound.'

And up on the platform came Ponder!

The children roared and clapped and shouted, and even William began to go pink all over with importance because Ponder had never looked so pleased with himself.

Ponder bowed to Punch; he bowed to Judy and the baby, he bowed to the policeman.

'Woof –' went Dog Toby, and Ponder gave him the biggest bow of all.

Then he jumped down into William's arms.

'Hurrah!' shouted everyone, for it was the best Punch and Judy Show they had ever seen.

Ponder's Song of Mr Punch

In scarlet and yellow,
  Scarlet and yellow,
In scarlet and yellow
  Gay Mr Punch goes.

Hat, jacket and breeches,
  Jacket and breeches,
All scarlet and yellow,
  And yellow his hose.

              Bright buttons of yellow,
                Buttons of yellow,
              Bright buttons of yellow,
                And scarlet his nose.

              Gay Mr Punch clad in
                Scarlet and yellow
              From the top of his head
                To the tips of his toes.

Ponder Gets the Dinner

The sun was shining but the wind was blowing so hard that Cousin Winifred said it was too cold for them to take a picnic lunch on the beach as usual. Instead, she said they could stay in the garden, which was warm and sheltered, and have dinner in the summer-house.

'Dinner in the summer-house!' exclaimed Ponder, his eyes growing shiny bright. 'Ha, ha, I should like that.'

William liked it too, and when Cousin Winifred said they could get the dinner ready themselves while she sat in one of the striped chairs on the step of the summer-house, Ponder and William were so excited that they did a song and dance all round the kitchen.

It was Hector the parrot's tune, and it went like this –

'Cock-a-doodle-doo,
Shepherd's pie and stew,
We're going to get the dinner ready
And we know what to do.'

When they had danced round the kitchen table twice and were sitting on the floor to get their breath back, Cousin Winifred said that they were not having shepherd's pie or stew for dinner. She said there was corned beef, already taken out of its tin, hard-boiled eggs which she had boiled with their breakfast eggs that morning, tomatoes, a lettuce which needed washing, young, raw carrots which needed scrubbing, brown bread and butter, fruit salad and ice-cream. All that they had to do was to lay the table in the summer-house, wash the lettuce and carrots, arrange everything on a tray and carry it into the garden.

She picked up her sunglasses and went outside.

Alone in the kitchen, Ponder and William gazed at each other with pleased smiles.

'You lay the table,' said Ponder. 'I don't know which way the knives and forks go.'

'You wash the lettuce and carrots,' said William.

'And we'll both carry the tray,' said Ponder.

William took a table cloth from one drawer, a handful of spoons, knives and forks from another and ran off into the garden.

Ponder rubbed his paws together, picked up Cousin Winifred's cotton apron and tied it round his chest.

'Now, lettuce and carrots,' he said, marching up to the vegetable rack.

Ponder was very fond of carrots, especially young, raw ones. Once he had even gone into Cousin Winifred's vegetable garden, and walked down the rows of young carrots pulling them up and eating them as he went. William had been very cross with him, until William decided that he too liked young, raw carrots, and now whenever they were with Cousin

Winifred, she always gave them young, raw carrots with their cold dinner as a treat.

'Ugh – dirty,' Ponder grunted as he looked at the bundle of carrots in his paw, and 'Very dirty,' as he

lifted up the lettuce on which there were several green-fly.

'Hot water and soap powder,' he said, marching over to the sink. 'That's the way to wash things that are dirty.'

As he wasn't tall enough to reach the sink, he drew

up a stool and stood on that. Then he turned on the
tap – whoosh – the water shot into the washing-up
bowl, hit a spoon and showered all over him.

'Grr – whirra-whirra-whirra-whirra,' he went,
trying to shake himself dry and wipe his eyes with the
apron.

He took the spoon out of the bowl, carefully
shook nearly half a packet of washing powder into
the bowl, filled the bowl with steaming hot water,
and stirred the froth with his spoon.

'A-tishoo –' he sneezed, as the washing powder
tickled his nose.

He threw in the lettuce, carrots and scrubbing
brush, and stirred again. The foam rose higher and
higher; it covered the spoon, his paws, the taps in the
sink; it touched his chest and his chin.

'A-ishoo –' sneezed Ponder, and the foam flew off
his chin and hit the window. 'A-isoo-ishoo-a-tishoo –'
It stuck on his nose and his ears, and the more he
tried to flick it off, the more it stuck, to the top of his
head and the back of his neck. 'A – ti – shoo –'

William came running in from the garden.

'I've laid the table and –' he stopped and stared.

'What are you doing, Ponder?' he asked.

'Wad – wad – waddig – ashoo – the carrods,'
sneezed Ponder, sounding as though he had a bad
cold because his nose was full of foam.

He turned round and smiled at William, his black
eyes gleaming through the froth.

'Ad the lettuce,' he said.

'Ponder –' stammered William, 'not in washing powder?'

'Yed,' said Ponder happily. 'They were very dirdy – like clodes.'

'But – but where are they?'

'Id in the wader.'

'But where's the water?'

'Udder the foab.' Ponder dived with his spoon into the froth.

William ran to the sink and peered into the white mountain. Ponder slowly drew up a wilted, steaming lettuce.

'No greedfly, now,' he said.

He dived again for the carrots, but they wouldn't be caught. They slid in and out of the spoon like gold-fish.

Ponder mopped his face with the apron. William turned on the cold tap to try to get rid of the foam, but the foam rose higher and higher and began floating over the edge of the sink on to the floor.

'We'll have to take the foam away,' William cried, turning off the tap.

He seized the milk saucepan from the stove and scooped up a saucepan full of foam. Ponder jumped off his stool and seized his sandcastle bucket.

Together, puffing backwards and forwards, they emptied the foam in a pile outside the kitchen door, where it sparkled in the sunshine like a summer snowman. They put the lettuce on top of it.

'We can eat the carrots even if they do taste soapy,' said William.

He picked up a tray and three plates. Ponder heaped on the corned beef, carrots, eggs and tomatoes. William put on the loaf of bread and the butter dish.

'We'll come back for the fruit salad and ice-cream and orangejuice to drink,' he said.

Ponder took off Cousin Winifred's apron and wiped the last speck of foam from his fur.

'How do you wash lettuces?' he asked.

'In water,' said William. 'Cold water with salt in it.'

'Oh,' Ponder looked thoughtful. 'Not like clothes?'

'Not like clothes,' said William firmly.

And each taking an end of the tray they marched out into the garden towards the summer-house.

Ponder's Song of the Foam Sea Horses

White horses,
Sea horses,
Horses that ride
Cantering up on the incoming tide.

White horses,
Sea horses,
Horses of foam
Riding the waves to come galloping home.

A Trip in the Mary-Anna

One afternoon Ponder and William were sitting on the beach watching the boats out at sea. There were the shining green and white steamers going backwards and forwards to the pier; there were sailing-boats with red, blue, yellow and white sails – Cousin Winifred said the ones with red sails were called Redwings – there were motor-boats, canoes, and there were the white rafts being paddled out from the sands near the pier.

'I wish we could go on one of those rafts,' said Ponder.

'So do I,' said William, and he turned round to ask Cousin Winifred if they could.

But for once Cousin Winifred said No. She said they mustn't go on the sea alone. They might paddle away so far that she would have to swim out after them and get all her clothes wet. She said she would take them to the boating-lake where it would be quite safe for William to have any sort of boat he wanted and paddle it there for as long as he liked.

'A real boat – to ourselves?' asked Ponder. 'No one else in it at all?'

'No one at all,' said William happily.

'Not even a Captain?' asked Ponder.

'I'm going to be the Captain,' said William. 'And you can be the crew.'

'O-oh,' grunted Ponder, because he rather liked the idea of them being Captain and crew of their very own boat.

The boating-lake was long and narrow. At one end there was a piece especially for sailing toy boats; in the middle, there was room for rowing-boats and canoes, and at the other end there was a piece especially for boats for children.

'It's like being on the sea really,' said William, when they saw the lake rippling in the wind. 'It's sea water and there are bits of seaweed in it.'

He and Ponder stood looking at the small boats in the children's piece while Cousin Winifred talked to the man who was hiring them out. They had names

like Lucy-Anna, Mary-Anna and Sally-Anna, and they were all brightly painted, green and white, blue and white, yellow and white, red and white. There was only one red and white, the Mary-Anna, and of course William knew that that was the one Ponder wanted.

'I do hope she asks for it,' Ponder whispered. 'She must ask for it, William – oh dear –' and Ponder was so upset in case he did not get the Mary-Anna that he turned his back on the boating-lake and stared hard at a seagull on the wall.

But Cousin Winifred did ask for the Mary-Anna and at last Ponder and William found themselves sitting on the shining white seat in it rocking gently up and down.

Ponder looked at the water. It was very high and close. He had only to put his paw out and he could touch it. He looked at the water again – it was even higher than his feet, in fact his feet in the bottom of the boat seemed to be under the water. Hurriedly he looked at his feet to see if they were getting wet, but they weren't, and Ponder smiled to himself – the water was outside and he was inside, so there was nothing to worry about.

'How does it go?' he asked William. 'There aren't any oars or a sail and it doesn't seem to have a purr like a steamer.'

'It paddles,' said William. 'There's a handle by you and a handle by me, and if we turn the handles the boat paddles itself along.'

Ponder grasped his handle in both his paws. William grasped his handle.

'Turn!' he shouted.

They turned.

'We're moving!' Ponder cried. 'We're moving!'

'I'm Captain,' called William. 'Full speed ahead!'

The red and white paddles glittered in the sunshine as the Mary-Anna splashed forward and zigzagged across the boating-lake.

'You try turning both handles, Ponder, and I'll be a real Captain and watch where we are going,' said William.

He slid off the seat and crouched down in the bottom of the boat, shading his eyes with his hand.

Ponder wriggled into the middle of the seat, grasped both handles and turned as fast as he could.

'Land ahoy!' shouted William.

'Ay, ay, sir,' said Ponder, because he was sure that was what sailors always said.

'Land ahoy!' shouted William again, as the bank of the boating-lake came nearer and nearer.

'Ay, ay, si—'

'We're going to hit the bank – stop her – Ponder – stop her!' William shouted.

'How? There aren't any brakes,' squeaked Ponder, poking about with his feet because he knew that was where motor-cars had their brakes.

'Boats don't have brakes,' William cried, and he sprang on to the seat and seized a handle from Ponder.

'Paddle backwards,' he shouted.

'Eh?' said Ponder, watching the spray flying from the sides of the Mary-Anna.

'Backwards!' cried William.

'Backwards,' repeated Ponder, and went on turning forwards as hard as he could in his excitement.

What with William turning his handle backwards and Ponder turning his handle forwards, the boat started going round and round in circles faster and faster.

'We're moving – and we've not hit the bank!' panted Ponder.

'STOP!' William shouted – and stop they did, so suddenly, that the Mary-Anna jerked from the water and shot Ponder and William into the bottom of the boat where they lay on their backs with their feet in the air.

William began to laugh, then Ponder began to laugh. They were so helpless with laughter that even the Mary-Anna, who was rocking up and down on the lake, seemed to be laughing too.

At last they managed to pick themselves up and, grasping the handles once more, they paddled very carefully round the edge of the boating-lake past where Cousin Winifred was sitting – and Cousin Winifred was laughing.

'That is what is known as "catching a crab",' she called.

Ponder looked down into the bottom of the boat.

'Did she say we'd caught a crab?' he asked William, and he hurriedly tucked his toes up under the seat in case the crab came along and nipped them.

William nodded.

'Wonder where it went,' Ponder murmured.

'Don't know,' said William. 'But I don't think she meant a real one.'

'O-oh,' Ponder put his toes down into the boat again. 'Full speed ahead!' he called.

And the Mary-Anna splashed forward over the dancing blue waves of the boating-lake.

Ponder's Song of the Crab

Why does a crab walk sideways,
Sideways, sideways?
Why does a crab walk sideways,
When he wants to cross the sand?

Is the path too narrow,
    Or he too wide,
That he can't walk straight
    But turns to the side?
Does he think in his mind,
    As an old crab may,
That I can't be sure
    He is coming my way?
Though his eyes look forward,
    His claws I know
Are hurrying sideways
    To nip my toe —
    So —

Is that why a crab walks sideways,
Sideways, sideways?
Is that why a crab walks sideways,
When he wants to cross the sand?

Paper Hats and Carrots

The afternoon was warm and still and quiet. Ponder and William were lying on a rug on the grass under Hector's chestnut tree while Cousin Winifred was indoors changing her dress.

Ponder was lying on his back with his paper hat over his face to keep the sun off. His paws were clasped on his chest. There were bees humming in the honeysuckle round the summer-house and, although Hector was not up in his tree, a pigeon was cooing there and seemed to be saying –

'Tak' two coos Taffy,
Tak' two coos Taffy,
Tak' two coos Taffy, tak'.'

Sometimes he left the 'tak' off the end and sometimes
he only said 'Tak' two coos Taffy' once, but he said
it all so often that Ponder was beginning to wonder
if pigeons were always called Taffy and if they
always told each other to take two coos.

'Tak' two coos Taffy,
Tak' two coos Taffy, tak'.'

Ponder sighed happily, bees, pigeons, sun, the
wash of the sea at the end of the lane, and he was
nearly asleep.

Slowly his paper hat began to move across his face.
Ponder put up a paw and pulled it back. It moved
again.

'Go away,' said Ponder.

But whoever it was didn't go away and the paper
hat began to slide farther and farther back so that the
hot sun shone on the end of Ponder's nose. Ponder
opened one eye; he saw something soft and grey and
smooth by his left ear.

'Go away, Taffy,' he growled, thinking it was the
pigeon.

'Hee-haw,' brayed the pigeon.

Ponder rolled over and sat up in surprise for it was
a funny sort of noise for a pigeon to make – and it was
a funny sort of pigeon that he saw standing there. It
was very large, and greyish brown like a pigeon, but

it had four furry legs, two very long ears and a row of strong white teeth – and Ponder's paper hat was held firmly between the row of strong white teeth.

'It's a donkey!' gasped Ponder.

'Hee-haw!' brayed the donkey again, with his mouth full of paper hat.

'William! He's eating my hat,' Ponder cried, and he jumped up and tugged at the end of the hat.

William jumped up too, but it was only a tiny piece of Ponder's hat that came away when they pulled. The donkey slowly chewed the rest of it and then nuzzled his soft grey nose against William's shirt. William stroked him gently.

'I wonder where he's come from,' he said. 'He's not a beach donkey because he hasn't a saddle on.'

'He's lost,' said Ponder. 'He's lost and he's hungry. That's why he's eaten my hat. I think we ought to take him to the police station.'

Ponder had been longing to go to the police station again ever since Cousin Winifred had taken them there when they had found the ring in the shrimping-net.

'Come on, donkey,' he said, and tried to push the donkey towards the garden gate.

'Hee-haw,' brayed the donkey.

He lifted up his head and trotted away across the grass making straight for the summer-house.

'Come here, donkey, come here,' called William in a very fierce voice.

Ponder tried to whistle the donkey like a dog, but

as he had never whistled before he only made a weak, breathy 'phoo-oo.'

'There's plenty of air coming out but no noise,' he explained to William.

They raced over to the summer-house where the donkey had clattered up the step and was rattling about among the forks and spades. He seemed most interested in the lumpy sack in the corner by the lawn-mower.

'What do donkeys eat besides paper hats?' asked Ponder.

'Thistles,' said William. 'Thistles and carrots.'

'If we had some carrots and thistles,' began Ponder.

'He might come with us to the police station,' went on William.

'And I know where there are some carrots,' Ponder cried.

He scampered out of the summer-house, across the garden and into the kitchen. As there was no sign of Cousin Winifred anywhere, he took as many carrots as he could carry from the vegetable rack and scampered out again.

By this time the donkey had poked his head out of one of the summer-house windows and was nibbling pieces of honeysuckle, but – when he saw Ponder with his paws full of fat, orange carrots, he gave a great 'hee-haw – hee-haw,' backed into the shelf of bottles and jars, clattered down the step and ran after Ponder as fast as he could.

Ponder was so surprised that he forgot that that was what they wanted the donkey to do; he turned tail and ran too, round the garden, round the summer-house, round the chestnut tree with the donkey chasing after him and William dancing up and down in the middle of the lawn crying –

'To the police station, Ponder, to the police station!'

Then a carrot fell out of Ponder's paws; the donkey stopped running, Ponder sat down breathlessly on the grass and William flopped beside them.

'You should have run to the police station,' he began.

'Have a carrot,' said Ponder, and held a carrot under William's nose.

William took it and nibbled; Ponder nibbled and the donkey munched happily, wandering from one fat carrot to another.

They were still nibbling carrots when Cousin Winifred came out and found them. She said she thought they were very clever to have caught the donkey at all, but that there was no need to take him to the police station as he lived in a field on the other side of the lane; someone must have walked through the field and left the gate open, which was a very careless thing to do. She told William to stay in the garden with the donkey while she went to find the owner.

William stroked the donkey's soft nose as it nuzzled for more carrots.

'I like donkeys,' he said.

'So do I,' said Ponder.

And – 'Tak' two coos Taffy,

Tak' two coos Taffy, tak','

sang the pigeon
in the chestnut tree.

Ponder's Song of Thistledown

Purple for a king, dilly,
Purple for a queen,
Every thistle bears a crown
On stately heads of green.
Thistledown,
Dilly down,
Dilly down dilly.

Pillows for a king, dilly,
Pillows for a queen,
Feather pillows for a crown
The softest ever seen.
Thistledown,
Dilly down,
Dilly down dilly.

Ponder's Carnival

It was the last day of the holiday. Ponder and William were very sorry that they had to go home before they could see the Island Carnival the next week. Cousin Winifred said that in the Carnival everyone dressed up in fancy dress, all the lorries, cars and bicycles were dressed up, too, and went slowly through the streets in a long procession, while everyone who did not want to dress up stood on the pavement cheering and waving. The Carnival procession usually ended up in the dark on the boating-lake where there were fairy lights round the water and fireworks set off from the boats floating there.

Even Hector the parrot was going to be in the Carnival on a lorry called Treasure Island, with cardboard palm trees, boxes of treasure and boys dressed up as pirates. Hector was going to be the pirates' parrot.

'All pirates have parrots,' William explained to Ponder as they walked up the lane together from the sea on their last evening.

Ponder's spade went clink-clink-clink behind him as he trailed it on the stones.

'I wish we could have a Carnival of our own,' he said.

'So do I,' said William. 'But we haven't got fancy dress or a bicycle or a car – not even a lorry.'

'Or fireworks,' said Ponder.

They walked on without saying a word. Clink-clink-clink went their spades on the ground and overhead where the branches of the trees almost met across the lane, the sky was growing pink in the evening light.

When they were nearly at the garden gate, Ponder stood still. His black eyes were shiny bright.

'But – we have got the wheel-barrow,' he said.

William stopped and he smiled.

'In the summer-house?' he asked.

Ponder nodded. 'It could be anything – anything we liked.'

'A boat,' said William. 'I should like it to be a boat – the Mary-Anna –'

'Or a motor-boat,' said Ponder.

'Or a green and white steamer,' added William.

'A green and white steamer,' said Ponder. 'I should like that best of all.'

They dropped their buckets and spades inside the gate and ran across the grass to the summer-house.

'It's green,' William cried to Ponder. 'The wheel-barrow is all green and so that will make the bottom part of a green and white steamer.'

Carefully they pulled the wheel-barrow out on to the lawn and dusted it with William's handkerchief.

'Now,' said William, holding up his hand and counting on his fingers, 'we want a funnel –'

'Red,' said Ponder, because all the steamers had red funnels.

'And two masts, one at each end, and – a white part for the funnel to sit on and – that's four.'

'And a flag,' said Ponder. 'We must have a flag like Cousin Winifred's kitchen towel and then it can be the steamer we came over on to the Island.'

'Five,' said William, and he counted on his fingers again. 'A funnel, a white part, two masts and a flag.'

'We could use my packing-case for the white part,' said Ponder. 'It's not really white but it's hard and square.'

While Ponder scampered off indoors to fetch his packing-case, William walked round the garden looking for sticks to turn into masts. At last he found two that were not holding up any flowers, but when he took them back to the wheel-barrow they would not stand up on their own. As it was not his wheel-barrow, William did not think he ought to bang nails into it to fix the masts at each end. Then, suddenly, at the side of the summer-house, he saw three flower-pots. Each flower-pot was filled with hard, dry soil and in the middle of each flower-pot was a long, straight stick, and there was no sign of anything growing there.

William tucked a pot under each arm and carried them to the wheel-barrow; he put one at the front and one at the back. Ponder ran up dragging his packing-case and when they lifted it up, it fitted tightly between the flower-pots and held them firmly in place.

Ponder rubbed his paws down his chest.

'It's beginning to look like a steamer,' he said. 'Now we only want a funnel and a flag.'

'We can use my handkerchief for a flag,' said William.

The handkerchief was crumpled and grubby but when it was knotted on to one of the masts it looked very much like Cousin Winifred's kitchen towel.

'Now for the funnel,' said Ponder. 'I wonder if there is a large tin of red paint in the summer-house.'

But there wasn't. Ponder pushed all the jars and tins along the shelf one way and then he pushed them all the other way; he looked in every corner of the summer-house although he and William had swept it out and really knew what was there; he poked behind the lawn-mower; he looked under the table and chairs, but there wasn't anything large enough, round enough or red enough that could possibly make a funnel for the steamer.

'It must have a funnel,' William said thoughtfully. 'All steamers have funnels for the smoke to come out.'

'I thought it was steam,' said Ponder, 'like a kettle. Kettles steam, and I thought steamers steamed. Isn't that why they're called steamers?'

William didn't know. He said he would ask the Captain of their steamer when they went home next day.

'Do you think we could use a flower-pot for the funnel?' asked Ponder after a little while. 'It's round and red and if we put it upside-down it would be just the right shape.'

Ponder and William hunted all over the garden until they found the largest flower-pot there was. They stood it upside-down on the packing-case between the two masts, and at last the wheel-barrow looked like a green and white steamer.

Ponder scrambled inside on to the packing-case beside the funnel; William lifted the handles of the wheel-barrow, and slowly he pushed the green and white steamer forward.

'Tu-whup,' went Ponder, and 'Ting-ting – ting-ting,' as they moved round the garden.

'I'll call Cousin Winifred to be the people watching the Carnival, and we'll go round again,' said William.

So Cousin Winifred came out and stood by the summer-house waving and cheering – but – Cousin Winifred had a very special surprise for Ponder and William. Out of her handbag she took a long, thin packet and a box of matches – and what do you think was in the long, thin packet? Yes, fireworks, little

sparklers that could be held and waved in the growing dusk.

William put some in Ponder's paws where he sat
in the steamer; he poked some in the flower-pots
holding the masts until the whole steamer was
sparkling with light. Then he pushed the Carnival
wheel-barrow round and round the lawn.

'I'm sure this is a better Carnival than the one next
week,' he called to Cousin Winifred as he went past
for the fifth time.

At last the sparklers died down, the wheel-barrow
was tucked away in the summer-house, and William
went to the gate to pick up their buckets and spades.

Ponder looked at the garden where the sun had set
behind Hector's chestnut tree. It was something like
Cousin Winifred's garden at home, and he could
almost see Cousin Winifred's three cats, Tigger,
Ginnie and Marmalade sitting on the grass waiting
for the moths to flutter out in the half light.

'I like holidays, but I like going home as well,' he
said to William.

'So do I,' said William happily. 'And we'll say
good-bye to Hector and the donkey on the other side
of the lane in the morning.'

Ponder's black eyes shone.

'We've got our packing to do tonight,' he said.
'Spades and buckets, shells and shrimping-nets.
Come on, William.' And they hurried indoors for
supper.

Ponder's Song of the Holiday

This is the case
I took on the train,
That puffed to the boat,
That crossed the sea
To the little stone house
With the chestnut tree,
That grew on the grass
By the garden shed.

Up in the tree lived
The parrot who said —
'Hello, hello,'
As I ran down the lane
Which went to the sand,
Where with shrimping-net
And bucket in hand,
I caught a ring
And a pearly shell.
There in the water
I paddled as well,
And found I could swim!

I saw the donkeys
And, in yellow and red,
Gay Mr Punch.
'Hello,' he said,
Just like the parrot
Who lived in the tree!

And under that tree
I made a boat
From the garden barrow,
And set it to float
Over the grass
In the fireworks' light.
A Carnival boat!

And now 'Good night' —
As I run indoors —
Is all I can say,
For there's not much time
At the end of the day
To pack the case
I took on the train,
That puffed to the boat
That crossed the sea
To the little stone house
With the chestnut tree.

About the author

Barbara Softly was born at Ewell in Surrey and she still lives near there. She took the Froebel training course and then specialized in History and English, and has had experience of children of all ages in her eleven years of teaching. She likes gardening, animals, and music, and attempts to play the clavichord. Her spare time is spent in keeping the three cats Tigger, Ginnie, and Marmalade, out of the goldfish pond and off her husband's flower beds. Barbara Softly has written three historical novels for boys and girls, as well as non-fiction, short stories, and articles.

also by Barbara Softly

Ponder and William

The first book about Ponder and William, in which they share weekend adventures throughout the year and Ponder does all sorts of other things as well, like going flying with a kite, painting himself as well as the garden seat, being chased by a hedgehog (which he thought was a scrubbing brush), falling into his own currant cake, and digging up all the lettuce seeds because he thought William had put them in upside down.

But Ponder wanted to be good, and William, who always *was* good, helped him as much as he could, and at the end of each gay and happy day Ponder made up a song to celebrate it.

*

Four of the stories from PONDER AND WILLIAM are available on 7″ E.P. records, told and sung by David Stevens, and issued by E.M.I. Records in their Playtime Series. They are:

Ponder at the Seaside
Ponder Flies a Kite   7EJ/257

Ponder and the Snow
Ponder and the Garden Seat   7EJ/258

*

There is also a book of six songs from PONDER AND WILLIAM set for unison voices and piano by Betty Roe, published by Novello & Company Limited.

Also published in the Young Puffin format

THE TEN TALES OF SHELLOVER *Ruth Ainsworth*

The Black Hens, the Dog and the Cat didn't like Shellover the tortoise at first, until they discovered what wonderful stories he told.

LITTLE PETE STORIES *Leila Berg*

More favourites from *Listen With Mother*, about a small boy who plays mostly by himself. Illustrated by Peggy Fortnum.

PADDINGTON AT WORK *Michael Bond*
PADDINGTON AT LARGE, PADDINGTON ABROAD, PADDINGTON MARCHES ON

Named after the railway station on which he was found, Paddington is an intelligent, well-meaning, likeable bear who somehow always manages to get into trouble. Illustrated by Peggy Fortnum.

THE HAPPY ORPHELINE *Natalie Savage Carlson*

The 20 little orphaned girls who live with Madame Flattot are terrified of being adopted because they are so happy.

FIVE DOLLS IN A HOUSE *Helen Clare*

A little girl called Elizabeth finds a way of making herself small and visits her dolls in their own house.

THE CASTLE OF YEW *Lucy M. Boston*

Joseph visits the magic garden where the yew trees are shaped like castles – and finds himself shrunk small enough to crawl inside one.

TELL ME A STORY *Eileen Colwell*
TELL ME ANOTHER STORY, TIME FOR A STORY

Stories, verses, and finger plays for children of 3 to 6, collected by the greatest living expert on the art of children's story-telling.

MY NAUGHTY LITTLE SISTER *Dorothy Edwards*
MY NAUGHTY LITTLE SISTER'S FRIENDS

These now famous stories were originally told by a mother to her own children. Ideal for reading aloud. For ages 4 to 8. (Six records also now released by Delysé, read by Kaye Webb.)

MISS HAPPINESS AND MISS FLOWER *Rumer Godden*

Nona was lonely far away from her home in India, and the two dainty Japanese dolls, Miss Happiness and Miss Flower, were lonely too. But once Nona started building them a proper Japanese house they all felt happier. Illustrated by Jean Primrose.

THE STORY OF FERDINAND *Munro Leaf*

The endearing story of the adventures of the nicest bull there ever was – and it has a very happy ending.

MEET MARY KATE *Helen Morgan*

Charmingly told stories of a four-year-old's everyday life in the country. Illustrated by Shirley Hughes.

LITTLE OLD MRS PEPPERPOT *Alf Prøysen*
MRS PEPPERPOT TO THE RESCUE
MRS PEPPERPOT IN THE MAGIC WOOD

Gay little stories about an old woman who suddenly shrinks to the size of a pepperpot.

DEAR TEDDY ROBINSON *Joan G. Robinson*
MORE ABOUT TEDDY ROBINSON

Teddy Robinson was Deborah's teddy bear and such a very nice, friendly cuddly bear that he went everywhere with her and had even more adventures than she did.

CLEVER POLLY AND THE STUPID WOLF *Catherine Storr*

Clever Polly manages to think of lots of good ideas to stop the stupid wolf from eating her.

THE ADVENTURES OF GALLDORA *Modwena Sedgwick*

This lovable rag doll belonged to Marybell, who wasn't always very careful to look after her, so Galldora was always getting lost – in a field with a scarecrow, on top of a roof, and in all sorts of other strange places.

DANNY FOX *David Thomson*
DANNY FOX MEETS A STRANGER

Clever Danny Fox helps the Princess to marry the fisherman she loves and comes safely home to his hungry family (*Young Puffin Originals.*)

LITTLE O *Edith Unnerstad*
THE URCHIN

Enchanting stories of the Pip Larsson family.

LITTLE RED FOX *Alison Uttley*

Little Red Fox is adopted by kind Mr and Mrs Badger, but finds it hard to be as good as their own children.

GOBBOLINO THE WITCH'S CAT *Ursula Moray Williams*

Gobbolino's mother was ashamed of him because his eyes were blue instead of green, and he wanted to be loved instead of learning spells. So he goes in search of a friendly kitchen. Illustrated by the author.

ADVENTURES OF THE LITTLE WOODEN HORSE
Ursula Moray Williams

To help his master, a brave little horse sets out to sell himself and brings home a great fortune.